CW01499313

THICKER THAN BLOOD

MILA CRAWFORD

MILA CRAWFORD

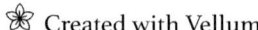 Created with Vellum

AUTHOR NOTES

Please be advised this book has a content warning. If you are a sensitive reader please proceed with caution.

- Domestic violence (In the Past off page. FMC)
- Degradation
- Primal Play
- Impact Play
- Bond@ge
- Depictions of violence and violent acts.
- Play with red human fluid
- Play with sharp objects that are used to cut up fruits, vegetables and meat
- DVP
- DP

-Spit play

-C*m play

=Pegging

-@nal

-Public sexual acts

-Fisting

PROLOGUE

Three Months Ago

Alexie

THE COLD AIR hits me as I stumble out of the bar. My fourth consecutive night of drinking myself stupid. I reflect on ending it all because life is a bleak loop of bullshit.

My brother tells me I need to get laid or beat the shit out of someone, and I'll snap back, but the truth is, I'm not interested in either. I want to float in blackness and not ponder on shit.

"You should come around more often, man. You're hilarious," some random guy says as he pats me on the back.

I smile and wave my hand while my stomach churns, and the bile of too much alcohol and not enough food moves up my esophagus. It's fuckin' easy to be liked by random frat boys at bars. I pull out the black card and load them up with alcohol, which brings the girls, and everyone has a good time. Good old Alexie, always the life of the party. They don't see what's in my head—depraved, fucked up darkness.

My lungs expand with the air I don't want to breathe as I walk to my bike. It'd probably feel good to crash it against the side of the building I just left. My boys say I'm too destructive, and they're partly right. I wasn't always this way, but ten years of the shit I've seen has a way of twisting a man's insides until he craves nothing but the empty blackness.

My feet shuffle on the pavement as if on autopilot, moving because they have to, not because I will them to.

"I'm not interested. Get the fuck off me!"

I turn my head toward the source of the voice—a woman barricaded by a giant man. His arms are on both sides of her head, covering her with his frame and blocking her from my view as he cages her in. I can see her red heels moving awkwardly against the ground before one lifts, and the man stumbles back as she knees him in the balls.

Ouch, that's gotta hurt.

She stands over him, hands on her hips, a fierce look on her majestic face. "Letting you buy me a drink in the bar doesn't mean you get to bang me beside a dumpster, you stupid prick."

My lips turn up in a smile, and for the first time in a long time, it's not forced. I can't help my sense of exhilaration at seeing this woman taking no shit from a man more than twice her size. I don't think many men could hold their own against a guy this fuckin huge, but there she is, refusing to cower down, head held high, dignity in hand, and ready for battle.

My cock twitches as I stare at the Black goddess. Her skin's a perfect shade of umber, her dark, tight curls framing her pretty face as her amber eyes blaze with fury. And her body—Jesus, it's a sin to have a body like that. She's tall, with huge breasts, thick thighs, and a round stomach any sane man would want to sink his teeth into. I'd never say no to having her legs wrapped around my waist or neck. She's a vision. If the perfect-looking woman exists, there she stands.

An average man wouldn't get a hard-on as he watches a beautiful woman attack a man twice her size, knowing it might not end well for her. But I never claimed to be an average man.

"You little bitch," the guy spits.

He gets up, one hand grabbing his crotch while the other dives into his pocket and pulls out a switchblade.

My fingers wrap around my gun, tucked in the back of my black jeans. If this fucker thinks I'd let him hurt her, he's got another thing coming.

He flicks the knife open, and the goddess's eyes widen. "I was gonna have a little fun with you. You would've enjoyed it. Now I'm gonna fuck you while I cut off your fucking s, you dumb cunt."

Rage. All I see is complete rage. I've spent ten years of my life hunting men like this who degrade, humiliate, and force people into sexual servitude. During that time—helping my brother look for his woman—we helped a lot of victims escape situations like this: abusive husbands, pimps, and sex trafficking rings. There's no fucking way I'll stand by and watch this motherfucker hit or rape a woman, use her like she's fucking nothing.

The goddess moves away from him, her back pressed against the brick wall. "Listen, you don't have to do this. You can walk away. I promise I won't say anything."

Her voice is shaking. The strong lioness is now a helpless kitten.

"Hey, what's going on here?" I walk over to them, getting right up to the guy's face.

The fucker flinches, pretty typical for a coward, and that's exactly what he is for intimidating a woman.

"You deaf or something? I asked you a fucking question."

He blinks at me as if surprised I'd dare to talk to him. "This is none of your business, buddy. This is between me and this chick here."

My lips curl into a smile, one I'm told makes people uneasy. It's an image I've mastered over the years. Put them at ease before you slit their throat. I don't want this fucker to know I'm about to make his worst nightmare a reality. I don't want him to see me coming. "This is a private party, or can anyone join?"

His shoulders relax, and his filthy face becomes grotesque as he replies with a thin smile, "Hey, man, I've got no problem if you want my sloppy seconds, but I get to blow into this pussy first."

"Nah, bro, I'm not interested."

He shrugs his shoulders. "Suit yourself, but I'm getting me a taste of this pussy tonight."

"I can't allow that. The lady doesn't seem interested in whatever you're packing."

He turns to me, and his pudgy face grows red as his nostrils flare. One second passes, then another. The guy looks utterly confused as if he's not sure I'm talking to him.

He lunges at me with the knife, but I'm

quicker and point my gun in his face. "You shouldn't have brought a knife to a gunfight."

"Listen, man, why don't you walk away? This ain't none of your business."

The audacity of this motherfucker. He's got a gun pointed right at his face, and he has the nerve to tell me to walk away. "I'm making it my business."

His feet shuffle subtly. If you blinked, you'd miss it, but after years in the Bratva, I'm familiar with the tells that indicate fear. Killing men teaches you to recognize the moment they realize they've met the grim reaper.

His confidence wavers. Stupid as this guy is, he's not so stupid he thinks he can win a fight with someone holding a gun.

He moves back, his hands in the air, the knife no longer an immediate threat. "Sorry, man. I wasn't looking for any trouble. You know how it is. Friday night, and all that. I went out with the guys for a couple of beers, and this chick was a tease the whole night. She was flirting with me. I spent a good fifty dollars on her at the bar. You'd think fifty bucks would get me something. Too bad she was such a fucking tease."

This motherfucker. "Yeah, I get it. You see that car?"

"The Ford Focus? Yeah, why?"

"Walk over to it."

The fucker doesn't move his feet. He stands there, immobile like a fucking statue.

"I suggest you move unless you want me to blow your brains out right here."

His feet shuffle again, this time like he has rockets attached to the soles of his boots. I've never seen a man move so quickly, but you should never underestimate a scared coward. "I won't touch her. We can forget this ever happened."

"Take out your dick and put it on the hood of the car," I demand.

"I'm not into any of that shit, man. I don't want guys sucking my dick. I'm not gay."

"Trust me, that pathetic excuse for a cock is the last thing I'd ever suck. It's so pathetically small, I'm not sure you can even call it a dick."

"What the fuck is all this?" he demands.

"Take your knife and start slicing like you're preparing a cucumber for a salad."

Panic dashes in his eyes as they roam from me to the goddess. This fucker is pathetic enough to delude himself that the woman he was about to rape is now going to help him. Then again, maybe she will. She could be some bleeding-heart softy who preaches an idealistic notion that everyone deserves a second chance. Some people deserve a second chance, but not people like him who violate the rights of others. Not people selfish enough to believe their wants outweigh all else. All women need to know they're safe, and this fucker does not care about keeping them safe.

I'm not saying I'm a good guy. I know I'm not. I'm a piece of shit. A killer. My morals are a darker shade of gray, but one thing I'm not is a rapist like this motherfucker.

His hands shake as he lifts his semi-hard cock and puts it on the hood of the red Ford Focus. The knife he held so boldly not too long ago now stays limp in his fingers.

"Thin slices, julienne length, asshole." He doesn't move. I cock the gun. "Better hurry. I'm an impatient man."

The fucker holds the blade to the tip of his cock and screams as he slices. He looks up at me.

"Go on. One slice of cucumber isn't enough for a salad."

Blood spurts as he slices another part of his cock, then another. His screams echo violently in the night air.

"I think that's good enough. Something tells me you won't ever go near a woman again."

"I won't, man, I won't. Please have mercy."

"Oh, alright." I aim the gun between his eyes and pull the trigger.

I turn to face the goddess, but she's gone. Disappeared. I don't know why, but the idea of never seeing her again causes emptiness to bloom in my chest, stronger than ever before, which is saying something.

1

A lexie

I WALK through daily life in a daze, filling the emptiness with frivolous carnal desires to numb the ever-looming darkness known as loneliness. But no one wants to be around doom and gloom, so for the benefit of my adoring audience, I play the part of the loveable psycho. You can't walk around like an emo kid when your brother is the head of the Bratva. So here I am in a fancy sex club, wearing a ten-thousand-dollar suit, with a bottle of Gray Goose, ready to party.

THE DEBAUCHERY CLUB is a beautifully restored hotel in one of the most affluent areas in Chicago. The entire place has a speakeasy vibe. From the outside, it looks like a plain brick-and-mortar building. No sign, no glitz, no glam. But when you walk inside, you're transported to an entirely new world. Red velvet carpets and drapes and circular booths adorned with hand-carved wooden edges. The place looks like the kind of establishment Hemmingway and Steinbeck would frequent to discuss current events, not a tawdry sex club.

SEX CLUBS and strip joints aren't my thing. I don't have an issue with them, they just aren't for me. But you can't turn down an invitation from one of your best friends—the guy who'd take a bullet for you and have your back no matter—what when he asks you to check out his new pet project.

.   .   .

AXEL ASKED me to spend the night with them here, which is weird cause all they're doing is hanging over their girl, Stella. I stare across the table at Stella sitting on Kian's lap. Ronan's fingers are wrapped around her hair, and Axel is talking to me but doesn't make direct eye contact. All he does is stare at Stella. I don't know what's happening, but the men in my life are all dropping like flies.

I GLARE UP AT MIKHAIL. He's staring at the half-naked bodies gyrating on the dance floor. This is the only place where the white mask covering his face doesn't make him look like a crazy person. People don't dig someone walking around looking like Jason Voorhees or Ghostface. The comparison isn't too farfetched, considering Mik is an enforcer for the Bratva. The man's worn the mask since he was ten, trained by my piece of shit father to be name-less and faceless. Mik was a dispensable killing machine to my father, and he used him to take care of the unsavory shit he didn't want to dirty his hands with. Mik never talks about his past, his parents, nothing. I've known him for twenty years, yet he might as well be a stranger.

"YOU GONNA PARTAKE in the goods, Mik?"

"No," he responds, not looking at me.

KIAN GETS UP and stands beside him. Mik doesn't budge, standing there surveying the masses. I've always thought Kian understood Mik better than the rest of us. Maybe because they're both psychos.

"THIS ONE here says you've been a little destructive lately," Kian says loudly, pointing his thumb toward Mik, "So we thought what better place to bring you than a good old-fashioned sex club. You can get your dick wet, forget your woes, and hopefully, stop stressing everyone the fuck out."

· · ·

"Burying myself in random pussy isn't gonna fix shit," I say as I get up and head toward the bar.

There's no need for more booze. I've got two bottles of liquor at the table, but I don't want to deal with their shit anymore. I can't tell them I can't fuck anyone cause the only woman I want is the goddess I rescued three months ago.

I saved the woman's life, and she didn't even thank me. She disappeared, and all I had to show for it was blood on my expensive Italian leather shoes. It's not like she owed me shit cause she didn't. And to be fair, she witnessed a psycho murder a rapist. Bouncing out of there was the smart and sane thing to do.

That's when I see her, thick tight curls and a pretty round face. She's like a fuckin' dream, one I've woken from and am desperate to go back to. I know how insane it sounds, but she's taken over every corner of my mind.

.   .   .

SHOVING my way through the bodies by the bar, I hope to get to her before she disappears again.

SHE'S SPEAKING TO A COUPLE, if you can call them that. The man sits at the table with the woman on a leash beside him. Two bowls sit in front of her face, one with water and one with food. She doesn't have any utensils. Either slave and master or pet play. Not my thing, but who am I to judge? I've got my own messed-up issues when it comes to sex and what I like.

WHEN SHE TURNS AROUND, our gazes lock. I understand the panic fluttering in her irises because where I see salvation, she sees damnation. "Get the fuck away from me."

"WAIT!" I shout as I chase her through the crowd. "I'm not gonna hurt you. I just want to talk."

2

———

M IA

THE UNIVERSE HATES MY ASS. Hates me with a passion. No matter what I do, I can't catch a damn break. Three months ago, when I ran from the nut job, relief flooded my body in such a wave, it almost felt like I was reborn.

MY FEET MOVE SO FAST, I don't realize I've walked straight into my new boss, Axel Moretti. I've heard rumors about him from the other girls working here, but he's always seemed like a nice enough guy. Based on what they've said, I probably shouldn't have taken this job, but I need the money, and this place pays well. Med school isn't cheap, and I've got no desire to come out of it three-hundred thousand dollars in debt.

"YOU OKAY?" Axel appears concerned, but who knows how genuine he is?

"YES, I'm fine. Some guy was harassing me, so I wanted to get away."

AXEL PEEKS OVER MY HEAD. "Which guy? I'll get him booted out of the place. I don't need some drunk asshole harassing my staff."

"IT'S OKAY. I LOST HIM."

. . .

"WHERE ARE you running off to, Goddess?" the psycho asks, smirking at me.

"I SPOKE TOO SOON. This is the asshole who won't leave me alone."

"I'M NOT AN ASSHOLE. I'm a nice guy."

AXEL BARKS OUT A LAUGH. "He's nice like a wolf's nice before he bites off your hand."

THE PSYCHO GROWLS. A real growl, the sound a wolf makes, validating Axel's statement. "Get lost, Axel."

"MIA, this is Alexie, and I promise you, if he's chasing you, the last thing he'd ever do is hurt you. He might want to do other things to you, but hurting you is not one of them."

.   .   .

"WHAT OTHER THINGS?"

AXEL SHRUGS. "Probably X-rated adult things. But don't worry, from what I hear, he's very good, and ladies always come first."

"CAN you shut the fuck up, man?" Alexie says through gritted teeth.

AXEL LAUGHS and walks off to his table, leaving me alone with the psycho. "If you're worried about me saying anything, I won't. I want to be left alone. What sucks the most is I'm gonna lose my damn job."

ALEXIE COCKS his head to the side. "Why would you lose your job?"

I can't help thinking how sweet he looks. But all wolves can disguise themselves as sheep. "Because I'm not gonna put out for you. You'll run to your buddy, and he'll give me the boot."

· · ·

ALEXIE STEPS TOWARD ME, and I retreat until my back hits the railing at the VIP level. "Do I appear to be a mere boy?"

MY EYES ROAM his chiseled face with its five o'clock shadow, the rise and fall of his solid chest with each ragged breath, and the thick, brawny arms caging me in. My voice hitches as I whisper, "No."

"WHAT'S THAT, Goddess? Turns out you've lost your voice. Or do you need me to repeat the question?" He moves closer, his body pressed against mine. The man is packing serious heat between his legs. "Let me ask again. Do I appear like an insufficient boy?"

"No!" I shout.

· · ·

"REST EASY. No matter what you say, your job is secure. But I would like to make you an offer."

I'M NOT sure what kind of offer he has in mind, but as I stand here with his body pressed so close to mine, I'm not sure I could refuse any request this man makes.

I WANT to be the badass I know I am, kick him in the balls, and tell him to go fuck himself, but something about this guy throws me for a loop.

THE WAY his eyes roam over my body is so hot I could burst into flames at any moment. He licks his lips as if he's staring at a piece of Kobe beef and salivating for a bite.

BUT WHAT GETS me the most is how he looks at me with such intent and longing that it makes me feel majestic. There's heat behind his eyes, for sure. The man wants to fuck me, but wrapped around that heat is wonder, as if I'm the only one who can unlock the mysteries of the universe. No one has ever looked at me this way before. I didn't think it was possible to be seen the way this man sees me. But here I am, standing in front of a psycho, and he's looking at me like I'm the entire world. Talk about a serotonin boost.

"WHAT'S THE OFFER," I ask, my voice as shaky as my legs. The last thing I need is to swoon on the floor like some pathetic Disney princess.

"FIRST, WHY ARE YOU WORKING HERE?"

THE NERVE OF THIS ONE. "Why is that any of your business?"

"I'M NOT sure I like you working here." He glides his fingers to the thin strap of my corset. "I don't like all these men staring at you. It bugs me you're making their dicks as hard as you make mine."

WELL, *that just went from zero to sixty.* "Sir, I just met you. Well, formally. The last time I saw you wasn't exactly optimal. Who the hell do you think you are telling me what I can and can't do with my body?"

THE CORNERS of his lips turn up in a sly smile. "I'm the man who's gonna fuck you so hard you'll forget your name."

THE AUDACITY OF THIS GUY. "Moaning your name while you fuck me doesn't give you ownership of my body."

"SO YOU'RE gonna tell me why you're working here?" he asks, ignoring my statement.

"IT PAYS WELL, and med school is expensive."

. . .

"You're in med school? Could you be any more perfect? Ballsy, beautiful, and smart. It's like the trifecta." His tone isn't condescending; it's full of awe and admiration. The guy might be a psycho, but at least he doesn't seem to be a misogynist.

"Starting in the fall."

"It's going to be handy having a doctor for a wife."

"Excuse me?"

"I'll give you a million dollars if you let me do anything I want to you for a weekend. We can work out a contract, and I'll respect your hard limits. Nothing will happen if you say no upfront. Anything not on the 'no' list is fair game. Deal?"

. . .

MY FINGERS CIRCLE the glass of unattended alcohol at the bar. Without considering the repercussions, I fling it at Alexie, watching as the amber liquid glides down his handsome face. "What the actual fuck? I'm not a hooker, asshole."

HE STEPS BACK, laughing as he dries his face with a handkerchief. "That little stunt makes me want to fuck you more. I appreciate women who love to fight."

"ARE you so arrogant you assume you can buy anyone or anything? Must be nice to be that rich."

"I DON'T CONSIDER it as buying you."

"WHAT THE HECK do you think offering me a million dollars for sex is?"

. . .

"I'm gonna fuck you either way. I figured this way, you'll be able to pay your tuition and not have to work here."

"What if I want to work here?"

"I'm a jealous man, Mia. You've seen how crazy I am. You want to have the death of multiple men on your conscience?"

"You're deranged," I spit.

"Yes, but how deranged I get is up to you."

It's insane to be so into an unhinged guy, but damn, he's hot. Not average hot. Scorching. He makes movie stars look like dogs in comparison. And it's flattering to have someone go a little deranged because they crave you so much. It's also been forever since I had sex. It's getting to where I'm worried if it's like riding a bike or if you don't use it, you lose it.

I LIFT MY CHIN. "If you want me to submit, you're gonna have to give me more than money."

"OKAY, WHAT DO YOU WANT?"

"TO FUCK YOU UP THE ASS."

ALEXIE SMIRKS, pushing up against me again. "That's all? Cause, baby, I'd do anything for a chance to fuck your sweet pussy."

"AND I WANT THE MILLION DOLLARS."

.   .   .

"GODDESS, you can have all my money. This is how I get my foot in the door, and I don't plan on leaving."

"YOU'RE AWFULLY FULL OF YOURSELF."

HE WINKS. "Soon, you'll be full of me, too."

3

A Maxie

"I DON'T WANT her working here anymore," I blurt to Kian.

MY EYES FOLLOW Mia as she moves through the bar, and my fingers itch to strangle every fucker who dares to look down her shirt.

"YOU CAN'T KILL anyone here, Alexie," Kian warns, his eyes on my closed fists.

"I NEED you to go tell her she's done for the night," I demand.

"I DON'T KNOW who the fuck you think you're talking to, but I don't take my orders from you. The only person at this table who can tell me what to do is that pretty girl with dark hair," Kian says, pointing to Stella.

STELLA TURNS as if sensing Kian's eyes on her. It must be nice to be so in tune with another human being that you can communicate without words.

STELLA SMILES SWEETLY and scoots toward Kian. "You being a bad boy, Kian?"

. . .

KIAN LAUGHS, a sound I'd never heard until Stella came into his life. His fingers inch along the table, and he picks up the steak knife. Pressing it into her flesh, he drags the tip slowly along her cleavage, drawing the slightest amount of blood. Dipping his head, he sticks out his tongue and laps at the trickle of crimson fluid. "I'm always a bad boy, sweet girl. But that's what you like about me."

"KIAN, tell her she can have the night off with full pay," Stella gently encourages.

I'M EXPECTING Kian to grab her by the throat and do something Kian-like, but he gently kisses her forehead and mumbles okay.

STELLA'S DONE something to my boys. They're still crazy, and three men you don't want to mess with, but when it comes to Stella, they're three pathetic golden retrievers.

. . .

"DON'T WORRY. Looks like you're gonna be in the same boat soon, buddy," Ronan says with a sharp laugh.

"WHAT ARE YOU TALKING ABOUT?" I demand.

"YOU'RE ALWAYS RAGGING on the three of us and Max about how our woman controls us. But the way you're fidgeting and freaking out about that pretty girl over there tells me she's gotcha, hook, line, and sinker."

I WANT TO DENY IT, but the truth is, I'd take Mia to Vegas tonight and put a ring on her finger so damn fast if she agreed.

"LOOKS like I'll be the only man standing," Mikhail says with a low chuckle.

GOD, the fucker is freaky. He doesn't show his face, barely talks when we're out in public, and you never expect it when he opens his mouth, so it makes you jump out of your skin. It doesn't shock me that this man was my father's most ruthless enforcer. It's why my brother insists Mik be the one who accompanies me whenever I go anywhere because, apparently, I'm a loose cannon.

IT WAS ONLY that one time. I killed six people in a bar, but they deserved it. They were running a sex trafficking ring. One fucker offered me a seven-year-old for the night. Had I not been on uppers, I would've done a better job instead of creating a bloodbath in a public place. Max had to break a lot of heads and pay off a ton of people to keep all that shit under wraps. That's when I realized drugs weren't for me, and I've stuck to alcohol ever since.

I STARE at Kian as he speaks to Mia. She nods before turning her head toward me with a smile, but it's not sweet or kind—it's a smile that tells me she'll make me pay. I've never been the guy who submits to anyone, but the idea of being under her before I make her my willing victim gets my dick hard.

SHE WALKS TOWARD ME, the tops of her perfect, fat tits visible, making my mouth water at having them tied with rope. My cock threatens to bust through my wool pants at the thought of putting clamps on her pretty s and making her crawl on her hands and knees as she begs me to pound her tight cunt. I salivate at the notion of her yelling, *"Pound me, Daddy. Fill my tight pussy with your hot cum. Own me, Daddy. Tell me I'm nothing but your sweet cum dump."*

"STOP STARING AT MY TITS," she demands as she stands over me, a sultry smile plastered on her pretty face.

"STOP PUTTING THEM ON DISPLAY," I retort.

"READY FOR OUR BARGAIN?"

. . .

"HUH?"

SHE WINKS. "I get to peg your ass, and you get to fuck me like a blow-up doll for forty-eight hours."

"SO IT'S LIKE THAT, huh? No wining and dining, just some sixty-nine-ing?"

"YOU NEVER SAID I had to buy you dinner. The deal was one million dollars, I get to fuck your ass, and in return, you get to have me for a weekend. Kian said we can have a room upstairs. Neutral ground."

"YOU DON'T TRUST ME?"

"YOU MADE a man slice up his dick like a cucumber. Fuck no, I don't trust you."

.   .   .

"You've got a smart mouth. I can't wait to have it wrapped around my cock."

She places her hands on the table and leans over, pushing her tits together in my face. "Wanna see it sliding up and down between my tits before you gag me nice and good?"

I want to bend her over and fuck her in front of everyone. I get up and crowd her with my height. "You're playing with fire, Solnce."

My goddess doesn't even flinch. She smiles and places one perfect hand on my chest, leaning in and bringing her lips to the shell of my ear. "You might be fire, but you're about to meet kerosene."

4

MɪA

THE ROOM IS A PRETTY DUNGEON. White walls are adorned with silver designs. The smoky curtains are purely for decoration because there's no window to be seen. The bed is covered in white sheets, but above it are hooks, and in one corner, there's a table full of toys still packaged up with cleaning supplies for them.

IN THE OTHER corner are rope, cuffs, suspension materials, and spreader bars beside a frightening-looking St. Andrew's cross. The wall behind the cross is adorned with a selection of tools designed to bring pain or pleasure, depending on your poison. Crops, canes, paddles, whips, floggers—you name it, and it's probably stocked somewhere in this room.

I CALMLY WALK over to the table with the toys, trying to keep my cool even though my entire body tingles with excitement and trepidation.

ENDORPHINS ARE A SERIOUS THING, and all I can think about is how much I want to be railed by this man, a man I barely know, a man I witnessed kill another in cold blood. Yet even with what I know about Alexie, my mind seems to have shut off in favor of my whore of a vagina.

I TRAIL my fingers along the various boxes of strap-ons.

. . .

ALEXIE'S warm breath caresses my skin. "I've transferred the money to your account. Now, why don't you tell me what's off the table?"

"NO SCAT, no water sports, and no vomit."

"THAT'S IT?"

"I THINK SO."

"IF ANYTHING ELSE UPSETS YOU, say 'red.' I'm a piece of shit, but I'm not a fuckin' abuser."

I TURN AROUND and smile at him. "You said I don't get to say no."

"YOU DO. But the word is 'red.' Words like 'no,' 'stop,' and 'please' won't get me to stop. Only word is 'red.' You say it, and everything stops right away." He presses his fingers into my chin, lifting my head so our eyes connect. "You got it, Solnce?"

I NOD. My panties are drenched, and he hasn't even touched me yet. I'm not sure I can handle whatever he wants to do to me. This is the first time I've been so aroused talking to someone about sex that I think I might come on the spot. I don't understand what kind of weird spell Alexie has put on me, but it's so potent that I want to run.

THE HEADY MIX of obsession and desire can fuel or destroy you. I have no way of knowing what Alexie will do. Will he want me beyond reason so I'll become the most precious thing to him? Or will he want me so much that his passions will turn into insanity? Or will it be a combination of the two? The sane thing to do would be to walk away before we start anything, to wire the money back to him and have it be the end. But the way he looks at me pulls me in like a moth to a flame. Something about this man makes me not want to deny him anything.

"Good," he says, stepping toward me until his face hovers above mine.

His stare is unnerving, and I can't help but turn away.

Alexie growls, a visceral sound from some animalistic part of him. "Look at me, Solnce." When I don't move, his fingers tightly grip my chin, and he tilts my head up, his gaze burning into mine. "I'm a monster. I know what I'm capable of, but you're safe with me. You'll always be safe with me. No matter what we do in the bedroom, I promise you'll like every second. Do you have any idea how fucked up this is for me, too? I don't care about many people, Mia. It's hard to make me give a fuck. But for some fucked up reason, I'd burn my family to the ground for you. I don't give up my control, and I'm willing to give it up to you right now, in this room. You've unleashed something in me that wants to protect and ruin you for everyone but me. Don't deny this thing between us. It would be a mistake. I don't know many things, but whatever this is, it's something good."

I DON'T HAVE words because I trust nothing, not even how my heart constricts at his words, so I nod and lift one of the strap-on dildos. It's hot pink and not exactly small. "You think you're man enough to take this one?"

ALEXIE BARKS out a laugh before engulfing me in his muscular arms. "The measure of a man is what he's willing to do for his woman. And for you, I'd do anything."

"REST EASY, buddy. I'm not your woman."

SOMETHING akin to venom flashes in Alexie's eyes. He transforms from the gentleman of a moment ago to the monster from that night in the parking lot.

ONE HAND CIRCLES MY THROAT, and his fingers dig into my flesh while the other yanks my hair back with such force that I almost lose my balance. "Pay attention, Solnce. Make sure you hear me clearly," he growls. "I will be anything for you. I will crawl like a dog and worship at your feet like a deity. But I need you to understand this. I do it because you're mine. My woman. Mine."

I'VE BEEN HERE BEFORE, engulfed with a man so demented in his obsession with me he would kill me before letting me go. Alexie hasn't tried to hide his toxicity, and I swore I'd never fall into that trap again. "I don't want to be under anyone's control. I don't want to be told what to do, where to go, or who to talk to."

ALEXIE LOOSENS his grip on my hair, but his hand remains on my throat. A warning that he could kill me in the blink of an eye, and I'm too powerless to do anything about it. "I don't want to control you, Mia. Where's the fun of being with someone who just does what I want? I don't like weak women, Mia. That's not why I want you. When I look at you, I see strength, power, determination. Possession. That's what I want. To possess you the way you possess me. I want an equal, Solnce. I'm willing to give up control to you, Mia. Control I hold onto by a thread."

HIS WORDS whirl around my mind like a wild tornado. I'm lost in his voice, haunted by the desperate sadness lurking in his gray eyes. Men like Alexie are dangerous, much more so than men I've been entangled with in the past, but I can't help but believe him. I may be foolish in my willingness to succumb to this man, but I'm powerless to fight it.

"YOU'LL GET YOUR TURN, but right now, I'm the one with power, remember?'

· · ·

ONE SIDE of his perfectly full lips turns up as he lifts me upright by my neck. "Yes, Mistress."

"NO NEED FOR FORMALITY. Mia is fine."

"CAN I CALL YOU SOLNCE?"

I SHRUG as I grab the cleaner and spritz it on the pink dildo. "I don't know what it means, but I assume it's not bad."

"NO, DARLING, IT'S NOT BAD."

I TUG my hot pants down my legs, kicking them off my feet. Sliding into the strap-on, I insert the small end in my pussy and grab the remote control. Turning, I point my newfound cock at Alexie. I wrap my hands around the dildo as I watch Alexie's eyes glide down my body like a lover's caress. "Be a good boy and strip."

5

Alexie

I NEVER PEGGED myself as an exhibitionist, but I strip off my clothes one piece at a time in a slow, methodical manner while Mia soaks me in like she's starving and I'm the most decadent meal she's ever seen. Yep, my cock is rock hard.

I CAN'T TAKE my eyes off her hand as she strokes the pink dildo slowly up and down. Her hand glides along the shaft as her fingers pay extra attention to the head. I'm salivating like a damn dog.

IT'S a sad state of affairs when I'm jealous of a piece of silicone. I'm pretty sure at this moment, I'd be willing to chop off my right hand to have her touch on my dick.

I'M NAKED, standing in front of her, allowing her to have control, something I hold on to so tightly.

I'M NEVER this open with others. I've never allowed a woman to take the lead while I follow. The upper hand is something I enjoy. There's a sense of power that comes from people not knowing if you're going to be caring or turn around and snap their neck, making them nothing but a distant memory. Therefore, the role of the lovable psycho suits me well. Everyone likes me, but they also fear me.

. . .

SEEING MIA LIKE THIS, watching the fire in her eyes as she stares at the tip of my cock, gives me the power to relinquish control.

SHE RAISES AN EYEBROW. "You've got a piercing?"

"IS THAT A QUESTION OR A STATEMENT?"

"WELL, I guess it's not a question. I'm not blind. I can see the tip of your cock. There's a piercing or earring coming at me from all directions. Is it an earring? What do you call that thing? How long is it? I mean, you're thick! How'd it get from one end to the other?"

I LAUGH at her sudden nervousness. "It's called a magic cross. And trust me, darling, when I'm buried balls deep in you, you'll think you've died and gone to heaven."

. . .

I WATCH AS SHE SWALLOWS, her eyes wide.

"I LIKE you staring at my cock, but maybe you should check out the rest of the hardware."

HER EYES MOVE up to my chest. "Oh, god," she moans as her hand moves faster along the dildo. "You have pierced s, too? Fuck, that's hot."

"IT'S NOT THE BEST PART," I say as I stick out my tongue.

"ARE you trying to distract me? Are you hoping I'll get all crazy when I look at your metalware and decide I don't want you bent over taking it in the ass like a good boy?"

I OPEN MY ARMS. "I'm all yours, Mia."

· · ·

"Get on your knees," she demands.

My knees hit the cold hardwood floor without any hesitation, without protest or a fight. I relish someone else taking control—no, not *someone*. Mia.

My head is yanked back by Mia's fingers grasping my hair in a vicious act of dominance. Her eyes bore into mine, and all I can think is if this woman were God, I'd be the most religious man on earth. I'd devote my life to prayer and service in the hope she'd spread her legs and show me paradise.

"Be a good boy and open your mouth," she orders.

I've never been able to take orders well, but the demands falling from her lips might as well be sweet poetry.

.   .   .

MY MOUTH GAPES, and I wait for her to make the next move. The soft silicone slides into my mouth and my cock hardens. I'm not so much into the idea of sucking dick. The phallic-shaped silicone isn't what gets me going. It's more how she demands my obedience.

THIS ACT TAKES trust on my part. I'm sure my goddess thinks she's in control, but she's wrong. Her sense of power is a mirage created by me. I've allowed this. I could overpower her at any moment, take what I want, and rule her body with my brute force. But I won't because as much as I want to ravish her like a wild animal, there's something I want more. For her to trust me, to need me, to be so desperate for my touch, she'd do anything I ask.

I'M ALLOWING her to use my body so she can fulfill her fantasy. It's my first act of proving myself to her, showing her I'm worthy. It's how I'll work my way into every fiber of her being. It's the first step to making her mine.

6

M IA

ALEXIE'S LIPS are curled around the dildo, his eyes cast up at me, full of wonder. Once again, I'm lost in how this man looks at me. I now see why people want to be held in reverence with God because the power you receive when someone looks at you like you're superior to them is all-consuming.

ALEXIE GAGS as I push the dildo further into his mouth, and the piece in my pussy makes me shiver. Drool falls from his mouth as I pull out and push in again, moaning at the sensation. "You like taking this big dick, don't you?"

THE CORNERS of Alexie's mouth tilt up, but he can't smile because his mouth is so full. He simply nods and mumbles an incoherent word I assume is "yes."

MY EYES ROAM to his long, thick cock. The metal from his piercing shines as precum leaks from the tip and lands on the floor. My mouth waters at the idea of having his smooth dick deep in my throat, of him holding my head and fucking me into oblivion. I thrust my hips, slamming the fake cock deep in his throat, making him my bitch. His fingers dig into my ass as he pulls me toward him, encouraging me to move in deeper.

.   .   .

"SUCH A GOOD BOY. I think you deserve a treat."

A THIN LINE of saliva stretches from the tip of the dildo, connected to his mouth as I pull away from him. I use my heel to slam his fingers before they can move to his cock. I know he's desperate for relief but that happens when I say and not before. "Not yet, slut. You can't come until Mommy says."

ALEXIE LOOKS UP AT ME, doing as he's told, but the glint of mischief in his eyes tells me his mind is spinning. This is stupid. Here I am degrading a man capable of killing without a thought. I agreed to be his willing victim for forty-eight hours. What kind of moron agrees to that? What the actual fuck was I thinking?

"WHERE DO YOU WANT ME, SOLNCE?" he asks, breaking me from my thoughts.

· · ·

I GESTURE to the California king in the middle of the room. "On there, ass up."

THE BED SQUEAKS as he moves onto the mattress on his hands and knees, legs spread apart, muscular ass directed toward me, and his thick cock dangling, desperate for relief.

ALEXIE SHIVERS as I pour the lube along his ass and massage it between his crack. I've never fucked anyone up the ass, but my entire body shakes with anticipation. Once again, I'm taken aback by how sexy it is to see a man who holds so much power on his hands and knees for me.

HE SHIVERS as my fingers rub in the cool liquid. My thumb circles his asshole before I gently push my way in. Alexie clenches for a second before he relaxes.

.   .   .

"IF YOU CAN'T TAKE this tiny little thumb, how are you going to take this big pink cock?"

"I CAN TAKE anything you give me, Mia, but be careful you don't dish out anything you can't take in return."

THE GRAVEL of his voice is a direct hit to my clit. The way he threatens me, his voice cold and calculated, is frightening and exciting.

MY HAND GLIDES up the dildo, spreading the remaining lube on the silicone. "Pull your cheeks apart for me."

"FUCK," he moans as I gently work the cock into him.

HIS SHOULDERS SLUMP, and his head falls onto the bed. His moans are so damn hot, as is how his body molds and bends to my will. He's so strong and secure that he's willing to take this because it turns me on. The way he's accepting it makes me so damn wet, and all I wanna do is come.

"You like taking this cock up your tight ass?"

"Fuck, yes. I need to jerk off while you do this," he says, moving his hand between his legs to grab his throbbing cock.

I slap it away. "No." He moans as I grab his dick, working my way gently over his magic cross and up his shaft. "You don't get to touch your cock. You don't decide when you get to come. This is my time. I'm in charge here. You're my little bitch, got that?"

I apply force to his dick, and he moans in ecstasy. "That's it, baby. Work my cock for me. God, your hands are magic."

· · ·

HIS WORDS of encouragement force me to thrust harder in his ass. I want to make him climax. I want him to come undone while I fuck his ass and tug at his cock.

AN OVERWHELMING NEED takes hold of me, a desire for him to know I'm the woman who did this to him. I want him desperate for me and only me, for him to come so hard, he'll think he's lost his damn mind. I want him addicted to me, consumed by me.

I DON'T KNOW where this flood of emotion is coming from or why the act of owning this man's ass also has my heart wanting to own *him*. But here we are, a girl who only wanted a way to pay her med school bills, now needing a little more. The notion slices through my heart, and I'm lost in the sensations that a simple act of sex has unleashed.

PEOPLE SAY sex is important for the solid bonding of a couple. I've always thought it was bullshit, but as I hold on to this man's ass and revel in the control he's allowed me, my perception shifts.

No one has ever given themselves to me like this before. But this man, this killer, this psycho who allows no one to have the upper hand, has. This man has allowed me to have power.

This one act that was supposed to be meaningless fun has satisfied a need for him in me. The knowledge is frightening.

I move faster in Alexie, trying to outrun the emotion in my heart and the blooming hope of security in my mind. He grunts as I move one hand along his dick while the other tugs at his hair, pulling his head back.

"Grab the remote on the bed," I instruct, and Alexie reaches for the little black control. "Be a good boy and turn it on."

. . .

THE VIBRATIONS of the strap shoot through my clit.

"OH, GOD," Alexie moans at the added sensation in his ass.

"YOU LIKE THAT? You like how that dick vibrates in your ass, knowing I own you. Meeting my thrusts as I take your ass and make you beg for more." I move my hand faster on his shaft and hear him moan, bringing him right to the edge before I stop, denying him the release he needs so badly.

"GET your hand back on my cock, Solnce," he demands.

I PULL out of his ass and thrust quickly back inside. "I make the rules right now, not you."

. . .

ALEXIE GROWLS, sounding more like an animal than a man. "I'm going to pound your sexy round ass so hard you won't be able to sit down, Solnce. I'm going to make you feel me in every fuckin' hole for weeks. You'll be so sore that the memory of me will be embedded in every nerve ending. So, go ahead. Fuck my ass. Call me a good boy. Demand I call you Mommy. But know this, darling. I will fuck you so hard you won't see stars, you'll see galaxies."

I PULL AWAY, and not even a minute passes before Alexie's fingers are around my throat, my back on the bed, and his gray eyes staring viciously back at me.

Alexie

I'M DONE with letting her have her fun. My goddess let it go to her head, and now it's my turn to get what I want. From her.

HER BEAUTIFUL EYES round as I tighten my grip on her esophagus. "I warned you not to play with fire, Mia. Now it's your turn to open your mouth and stick out your tongue."

MIA DOES as she's told, and I move up the bed, my piercing gliding on her lips before I guide my cock into her open, waiting mouth. A hiss escapes me as she wraps her lips around my cock, engulfing me. She doesn't even have to do anything. Just being in any of her holes seem to be enough to have me on edge. I don't comprehend how this one woman can bring me to my knees when no other has.

HER FINGERS GRIP MY THIGHS, nails digging into my flesh as she scrapes them against my skin. "Yes, Solnce. Mark me as yours. Leave me a memory of how you choked on my cock like a good whore."

Mia sputters, her breathing labored. Fear flashes in her eyes. I'm confident she remembers what I'm capable of. I could end her so easily at any moment, but she doesn't realize I'm more likely to slit my wrists than hurt a hair on her head.

MY GIRL IS DIRTY. She's kinky. I can tell based on what she said was a "no" for her. Most girls don't ask to peg you. When she did, I learned she would be the one to unravel every feral, animalistic need in me. At that moment, she became my need, my obsession, my addiction, and my utter undoing. I've never needed anyone, but somehow, I need her. I can't imagine spending another fuckin' day of my life without her.

"Do you know what it's like to be so desperate for someone you think you're going crazy? Do you recognize how much your sexy body and slut mouth turn me on? That's why I'm doing this. You need to understand that you're mine. My slut, my whore. My everything. I own you like you own me. I want to corrupt you until you don't know where you begin and I end."

My cock twitches as her tongue swirls around the tip. She pays extra attention to my dick piercing, and the sensation is so powerful that I push further into her throat. She sputters and gags. It must be hard to breathe in this position, her head back with a thick nine-inch sausage lodged deep in her throat but my girl takes my cock as if her life depends on it.

"THAT'S IT, baby. Show Daddy what kind of cock slut you are. Look how happy you're making me, Princess. Gobble that dick like the good girl you are." I reach for the remote, moving it to full blast as she moans on my cock. "You need to breathe, Goddess?"

SHE NODS SLIGHTLY. "Then keep sucking, whore. Make Daddy come and you'll be able to breathe. Get me there like a good girl. Make your desperate, whore mouth useful, and milk my dick until I flood your mouth with my spunk. "

HER FINGERNAILS DIG FURTHER into my thighs. "Are you gonna come, Solnce?" I shut off the vibrator. "We can't have that, pretty girl. The first time you come will be on my tongue."

·   ·   ·

ANGER OR SPITE flashes in her eyes, and a moment later, her teeth graze against the sensitive tip of my cock. I can't help the spike of pride that hits me. Here she is beneath me, my hands on her trachea with the capability of ending her life, yet she has the nerve to warn me she can bite down on my dick.

I PUSH DOWN on her face. Her hands move from my thighs to my chest, and her body writhes under me. The sting of her teeth pressing further into my cock causes my balls to tighten. I pull out of her mouth and drain every drop of cum directly onto her cheek. She pants as I watch my cum slowly roll down her face.

HER EYES WIDEN as I bend to her ear and whisper, "Biting my cock won't make me stop. I like pain, Solnce. Doesn't matter if it's coming from you or me." My tongue darts out and I lick her cum stained cheek. "Why don't you show me how good of a slut you can be for Daddy and keep that pretty fuck hole you call a mouth open wide?"

.   .   .

MY TONGUE DARTS OUT, and I lick at her cheek, lapping up my cum and spitting it directly into her open mouth. "Swallow."

SHE CLOSES HER MOUTH, drinking me in before showing me her tongue as proof she's followed my command. "That's a good girl."

BEGRUDGINGLY, I move off of her before tucking her under my arms. "You okay?

"I DIDN'T SAY 'RED,' did I?" she retorts.

I LAUGH. I don't think I've ever laughed as much as I have with her. She seems to wipe away all the pain and darkness, and I like it more than I should.

.   .   .

"I DIDN'T GIVE you an out. It's hard to say 'no' when someone has your throat in a vice."

HER DARK EYES SOFTEN, and a sweet smile graces her face. Without a word, she flips on top of me, pushing my arms behind my back.

I'M IMPRESSED by her moves. The pink dildo's peeking between her legs and obstructing my view of her sweet cunt. She loses her balance when I wrap my legs around her waist and flip her, causing her to loosen her grip on me and freeing my arms. "I'm not sure you can get any more perfect. Where did you learn those skills?"

SHE TURNS her face away from me, answering my question with silence.

"I DON'T LIKE WAITING, SOLNCE."

.   .   .

"I GAVE you permission to take my body for forty-eight hours. I didn't say you could have access to anything else."

ANGER ROLLS off my body as I absorb her words. My teeth grind against each other as I glare at her. She thinks all this is about sex. "I didn't get you here to fuck you. I got you here to make you mine."

8

M IA

I'M ANGRY. This man assumes because I'm willing to fuck him. I'm also willing to crack open my entire life to him. He expects my vagina to be the key to my diary. One quick fuck, and *bam*, he knows it all. My secrets, my past, my hurts, my longings, my desires, my wants. But those are deep parts of me I don't share with anyone.

MY LIFE HASN'T ALWAYS BEEN easy. I've had struggles I'm not interested in sharing, especially with a man I barely know. A man who has the same penchant for evil, control, and manipulation as the one who left me with too many scars to count.

ALEXIE'S HAND moves down my body. It's as if he doesn't care we're in the middle of a conversation. Maybe he cares too much, and he's trying to distract himself instead of confronting me for answers I'm not ready or willing to give.

IT'S A SMART MOVE—BRILLIANT. He's looking to subdue me with sex, to break my will and resolve with his giant dick. Will it work? I want to think it won't. I want to believe I'm strong enough, that he can fuck me any way he wants, and I'll stick to my resolve not to tell him anything. But I also know he's a man who won't give up easily. No, he's a man who will *never* give up.

. . .

ALEXIE BRUSHES KISSES along every inch of my face apart from my lips; he avoids them, which infuriates me. Am I not good enough to kiss on the lips? He nuzzles my neck with a gentle brush of his mouth, and his hot breath makes my body clench with need and desperation.

HE PLAYFULLY NIBBLES on my lobe before his teeth sink in and he bites in warning. "If you don't tell me, Solnce, I'll fuck it out of you. And I'll tell you right now, you don't want me to fuck it out of you."

"YOU THINK THAT'S A THREAT?"

I FIND it humorous that this man thinks I wouldn't fuck him in every way imaginable for the rest of my life and die content. Does he own a mirror? He's built like a goddamn Greek God, yet with all the tattoos and piercings, he looks like he walked out of my wildest bad boy fantasy. And if that blow job is any sign of how this man likes to fuck, I'm pretty sure he'd put the devil himself to shame. So, if his only way of getting me to open up to him is by fucking me into oblivion, I welcome it with open arms.

A GUTTURAL GROWL escapes his lips just as he sinks his teeth into my neck. The room echoes with my scream. Fuck, that hurts. His teeth have pierced my flesh, and he's drawn blood. Perhaps I should rethink all of this like a sane person. But as I think I can't take the pain anymore, he kisses the spot and uses his tongue to soothe the wound.

THE BED SHIFTS as he lifts himself off his hands and stares at me. His steel-gray eyes burn with furious resolve, and the corner of his mouth glistens with a drop of my blood. He looks like a demon, a vampire, someone who's going to suck my soul out of my body, leaving me dry.

"IT'S NOT A THREAT, Mia. It's a fuckin' promise. When I said I want you, I meant all of you. I'm not content with the crumbs you're willing to give me."

I DON'T RESPOND because there's nothing to say. I hold my walls with sheer resolve, and he wants to knock them down with brute force. "You're wasting your forty-eight hours."

HE SHIMMIES DOWN MY BODY, keeping his weight off me. His hands move to my corset top, pulling out my breasts. I scream as he grabs my s between his fingers and uses them as leverage, lifting me off the bed. "These would look good with some jewelry, Mia. Hoops I can attach to a leash. Make you crawl like the pretty slut you are."

WET. I'm so fucking wet. I never thought I'd be the girl who's into degradation, but every filthy word Alexie says hits my clit without mercy. The need to come is so consuming that I might go insane if he denies me.

. . .

"Please," I pathetically beg.

"Please what, Mia? What are you begging for, my pretty little slut?"

"I need it."

"Need what? Use your big girl words. Tell Daddy what you need, so I can make it all better."

"Please, let me come."

Alexie doesn't say a word as he moves off the bed. He rubs his hands up my legs from my ankle, moving methodically until he reaches my hip. Hooking his fingers into the harness, he tugs it down my legs. "Spread 'em, slut."

My legs open for him, my pussy on display.

. . .

"Fuck, that's a pretty pussy. Use your hands and open up that wet cunt."

Heat creeps up my body from his hungry stare, his eyes full of longing and consumed with lust. The shiny ball on his tongue is exposed as he licks his lips. The way he watches me, while keeping completely still is pure torture. He knows exactly what he's doing when he cocks an eyebrow and crosses his arms over his chest.

"Are you just going to stand there?" I huff.

My hips jolt as his palm connects with my pussy. A fierce slap. It's meant as a warning. My body jerks, and I moan at the sensations, pleasure mixed with pain.

"It's my time, right? You got your part of the deal. If I want to just have your cunt on display for me for the next forty-plus hours, that's my right."

9

Alexie

I want to punish her.

Mia won't tell me everything, only allowing me to see small fragments, nothing of substance.

SHE RAISES her hips off the bed, offering me her pussy. My mouth waters, staring at her wet, open cunt.

SHE'S SO desperate for relief, and I want to take advantage of it. But what I want more is her heart, and to win that, I need her secrets. Her fears, her hopes, the darkness she hides, and the light she strives for. Every part of Mia will be mine, and I'm not ashamed to use my dick to get what I want.

"KEEP that cunt open for me. Remember, Mia," I warn, "be a good girl and get a reward. Be a dirty slut, and get punished. The choice is yours."

SHE SAYS NOTHING. I'm not sure if she's playing a game of submissive and dominant or waiting to figure out the proper thing to say to be the perfect little brat.

.   .   .

I GLIDE my fingers along the table of toys—butt plugs, eggs, vibrators. I grab a silver butt plug, bondage tape, a black dildo, and a bottle of lube.

"WHAT'S TAKING SO LONG?" Mia demands.

OH, she wants to be a brat. I discard the toys in my hands and grab the spreader bar and rope, dropping them on the bed. "Get up. "

SHE DOESN'T MOVE; she lies there, pussy exposed, daring me to eat her out. I gently caress her face, smiling at her as if I'm going to be sweet right before I grasp her beautiful hair and yank her off the bed. "When I say move, slut, you move your fucking ass."

SHE HAS the nerve to moan. She likes it when I'm rough, her s are pebbled, pupils dilated, and the smell of her sweet cunt, floods my senses like the most intoxicating drug on earth. The rougher I am, the hotter she gets.

"UP AGAINST THE WALL, spread your legs wide. I want easy access to my cunt. I'm gonna tear that pussy apart. When you're crying and begging me to stop, I'm gonna fuck you even harder until you wish you were dead."

I KNEEL in front of her, attaching one side of the spreader bar to one ankle before connecting it to the other. Grabbing the rope, I tie it around her waist, looping it toward her breasts, cinching them in a quick chest harness, making them look even larger. I want her bound up, completely at my mercy, at my disposal. She doesn't say a word, letting me work. "Remember your safe word, Mia. If you don't say it, I'll keep going."

"I'M NOT AN IDIOT."

.   .   .

OH, she wants to test me. My hand moves, and I strike her tit hard, making it bounce. She doesn't flinch. Instead, she pushes her chest forward, daring me to give her my worst. With the use of her hair, I toss her, watching as her ass bounces on the bed.

"HOW THE FUCK are you manhandling me like this? I'm two hundred and thirty pounds, and you just toss me here and there as if I weigh nothing."

"I BENCH press three hundred and seventy-five, Mia. You practically weigh nothing to me."

"HUH, I never thought I'd hear a man say that. My ex used to tell me how fat and disgusting I was."

I GLARE AT HER. Her words make me feral with the need to find the fucker and beat his head in until his brains splatter on the concrete. He's as blind as a bat cause every fuckin' pound on her body is mouthwatering and makes my dick hard as rock. Why would anyone not want that body? It's fuckin' sexy. Hard lines and muscles are not something I want to fuck. I want my dick buried in softness and my hands to roam curves. "I'm going to kill him."

"WHAT?" she shouts, panic lacing her words.

"I'M GOING to kill him. When we finish up here, I'm going to find him and kill him. I'll make it slow. He should suffer for hurting your feelings and die for insulting you.

"YOU'RE CERTIFIABLE," she snaps.

I DON'T ANSWER, opting to examine how she's bound up.

.   .   .

"WHAT ARE YOU DOING, YOU PSYCHO?"

REALIZATION DAWNS that her hands bound behind her back will give me limited mobility.

I QUICKLY RELEASE them and tie them above her head, moving the spreader bar to her knees so I have better access to her pussy and ass.

MOVING TO THE TABLE, grabbing nipple clamps, a riding crop and a few clothespins with a much lighter rope. I attach the clamps, one to each large, perfect nipple before turning my gaze to her pussy.

"WE NEED those cunt lips of yours spread wide so I can see you better." I pull her pussy lip and attach two clothespins and then tie them to the spreader bar at her knee before doing the same with the other.

.   .   .

"Jesus," Mia moans. "That hurts but feels good. How the hell does this feel good when it's not touching my clit?"

"Pain is interesting Solnce. It's a fascinating sensation. It can either bring earth-shattering pleasure or bone-crushing pain. I've spent a good part of my life exploring it, both on others and myself."

She shivers as I glide a crop down the center of her body until I reach the top of her pussy. "Such a pretty cunt. Big and juicy, like a fuckin' peach." I tap the crop on her clit. "And I love me some peaches."

"Please," she begs.

"Please what, Solnce?"

.   .   .

"You know what I want."

"You're gonna have to use your big girl words and tell me."

"You're an asshole."

I tap her clit again. "I know, but your cunt seems to like it. Did you know you're a filthy pain slut?" She doesn't reply, so I hit her again. "You gonna answer whore, or are you gonna sit there like a pathetic slut and let me beat this pretty cunt until it's sore and bleeding?"

Tap, tap, tap. I keep hitting her clit with the crop, harder and harder, waiting for her to use her safe word. But my Solnce takes it, even with the pull of her lips from the pins every time she finches or moves. I didn't think I could admire her more than I already do, but here we are. There's something to be said for someone who faces fire like a lion, brave, head held high, saying, "bring it." Fuck, that's hot.

"I'm not sure what's hotter, your pretty face, your sexy curves, or how you take it like the perfect little slut you are."

"I need to come, Alexie, please."

10

M IA

"I LIKE HEARING YOU BEG, Solnce. The powerful goddess turned into nothing but a pathetic whore. Your needy pussy glistening with desire, desperate to be used like a good little slut you are. Tell me, Solnce, are you a dirty slut? Is that what you are, a pathetic cum dump, my perfect little whore?"

I GRIT MY TEETH. I hate him, but I hate my pussy more cause the more depraved the things he says, the more turned on I am. If he called me these names outside of this room, I'd chop his cock off, but in this place, they're the hottest words I've ever heard.

"PLEASE, I NEED TO COME."

"I'LL LET YOU COME, slut, once you tell me what you are."

"I'M a girl who's ready to come," I spit.

"YOU KNOW what I want to hear, Solnce. If you want to come, you're gonna have to tell me
      what you are."

I SMILE, realizing that two can play this game. "I'm a dirty little whore. Please make me come, Daddy. Show my filthy pussy that only you can bring it pleasure. I need your tongue in my cunt. Please, Daddy. Please put your tongue on my pussy, like only you can."

THE CROP HITS the floor and Alexie falls to his knees. I wait in anticipation for the touch of his tongue on my clit, but instead, he pours cold liquid on my pussy. It slides down to my open and exposed asshole.

"WHAT ARE YOU DOING, ALEXIE?"

"GETTING YOUR TIGHT ASSHOLE READY, slut. I'm going to tear apart all your holes and make you so addicted to my fingers, cock, and tongue that you'll do anything for me. I'm gonna make you a junkie, Solnce. My perfect whore. Mine."

I SHIVER AS cold metal glides slowly through my folds and stops at my asshole. Alexie pushes the tip in slowly, allowing me to adjust. "You're doing good, baby. Just relax.

Daddy is going to make you come all over his tongue."

His praise is like a shot of heroin to my veins, an instant high I crave more than I ever thought possible.

I moan as he puts the plug in my ass, securing it with bondage tape I didn't see him carry from the table. Relief engulfs me because it could have been worse. He could have used duct tape. At least he had enough brains to realize that shit can rip off skin.

"That should do it." He tugs at the clothespins, and I jolt at the quick shot of pain. Before I can ponder the discomfort, his tongue is on me.

Fuck, his tongue! His tongue ring is the devil's work. The way the ball moves up my slit and focuses on my clit is sinful. Every man on the planet should get a tongue ring cause *hot damn*. I'm not sure what's happening as my body shakes. Tiny jolts of lightning spring through my nerve endings, and I'm lost in the confusion of utter bliss.

"OH, GOD," I moan as I arch my hips, desperate for more of the sensation from his tongue. "Why are you so good at this?"

HE DOESN'T ANSWER. Instead, he inserts one giant finger in me before quickly adding a second. He pumps into me as the tip of his tongue caresses my clit gently. I don't want him to be gentle. I want him to devour me like an animal in need. I want to know his hunger is at its peak and could destroy him.

FRUSTRATION ROLLS through me like the quick fall of a summer storm. "Please."

"YOU'RE A GREEDY LITTLE WHORE, aren't you, Mia? You don't like that I'm making you wait." He puts another finger in me, stretching me as he pulls back his tongue and slaps me directly on the clit. "Whores like you don't get to feel pleasure until they learn to be a good girl."

"PLEASE, ALEXIE. I NEED TO COME," I beg. He's right. I'm a whore, so desperate for relief I'll do anything he asks.

HE SLIPS his tongue on my clit briefly and adds a fourth finger. "Your pretty cunt is swallowing my fingers. You're such a good girl, Mia, letting me use you like a pathetic fuck toy."

COOL LIQUID CONNECTS with my open pussy, and I freeze. I realize what this man wants to do, and I'm a little frightened. "Don't, Alexie."

"THAT'S THE PROBLEM. You think you're more than my whore. You need to learn your place. I have to show you how much you need to be abused, used, and fucked so viciously that your pussy will weep with sweet cum at the mention of my name. You're nothing more than my whore. My fuck doll to use any way I want. Here, only for my pleasure."

A YELP ESCAPES my lips as he pushes his thumb inside me before his entire hand is in my vagina to his wrist. Moving in and out slowly before placing his tongue back on my slit, licking me with hunger and need. He makes tortuous circles around my clit, teasing me with the idea of release but never giving it to me.

"FUCK, YOU TASTE SO DAMN SWEET," he moans into my pussy.

"I NEED TO COME. PLEASE, ALEXIE."

HIS TONGUE RING slides around my clit as he uses it against that one sweet spot, twirling it until my hips rise. I'm almost at the finish line, desperate and wanting. As I reach my peak, he bites my clit, and I scream my orgasm, my entire being satiated.

HE DRAGS his hand out of my drenched pussy. It glistens with my desire and the depraved act he committed on me. I watch wide-eyed as he moves up the bed and stands over me. "Open your mouth for Daddy."

THE WORD DADDY is so taboo, so depraved, and so sexy leaving his mouth.

MY LIPS PART FOR HIM, and he shoves his fingers into my mouth with no warning. "Sample your cunt for me. Isn't it delicious, Mia?"

HIS ONSLAUGHT MUFFLES MY WORDS, and the only sound escaping my lips is the gagging from his fingers touching the back of my throat. "What are you, slut?"

. . .

I UNDERSTAND the words he wants me to say. He wants me to demean myself, to admit what we both realize to be true. Saliva forms when he pushes his hand further, giving my mouth the same treatment he gave my pussy moments ago.

HE PULLS HIS FINGERS OUT, a trail of saliva following it. "Say it, Mia, or I swear this time, I'll force you to take my cock and my entire fist in all your holes."

I BLANCH AT HIS WORDS, knowing full well he'll do it. I have a safe word to make this all stop, but using it means I'm folding, which would give him satisfaction. So instead, I close my eyes and whisper, "I'm your slut."

11

A

Maxie

Fuck!

When she bends to my will and calls herself a slut, I'm close to blowing my load. Not sure if I can last in her pussy. "What do you want Daddy to do to you?"

"Please, Daddy, fuck my pussy," she begs.

. . .

I WIPE the spit from my hand on her face, a pure act of degradation and ownership. She looks so pretty, lying there for me. Open, waiting, begging. "You're such a good girl, aren't you, baby? Does your sweet pussy need Daddy to stuff it with his big cock?"

"YES, please. Please, fuck me. I want to be your pretty whore, your good girl. Put all your cum in my tight little pussy."

SHE'S STILL BOUND UP, unable to touch me or move, completely at my disposal. She's so damn beautiful, soft skin illuminated under the moonlight. I fist her large bound-up tits in my hand, losing myself in my lust for her. Only for her.

"YOU'RE SO FUCKIN' hot, Mia. Every inch of you is a dream come true."

. . .

SHE WHIMPERS as I tug at the nipple clamps, and the sound makes my cock jerk. "Does that hurt Mia? Do you feel the sting of the clamps on your big, round nipples? Does that pain shoot straight to your juicy clit?'

"YES," she moans. "So good. I sense it all over my body."

I TUG the clamps again before moving down her body to stare at her open pussy. She's been a good girl, holding her legs still because every time she moves, those clothespins pull at her lips. Pain with her pleasure.

BENDING DOWN, I spit directly onto her clit before circling it with my tongue ring. I've never used my ring on another woman. I didn't appreciate why I got it when I did. Maybe it was the same reason I got my dick and nipples pierced. Pain. I wanted to feel something other than the emptiness I carried inside me for so long. My chest constricts with emotion for this woman. All I want is to love her, protect her, make her scream my name in the throes of passion.

I SPIT ON HER CUNT, my saliva trails down from her clit to her fuck hole. "Don't move, Solnce. Stay still while Daddy makes this pretty pussy sing."

MY HANDS TREMBLE with desire and need as I drag the plug from her ass and replace it with a black dildo. I press gently, letting her adjust before I have her crying out in pleasure. "Is that good, my pretty slut? Do you enjoy having your ass full?"

"YES. Oh, yes. Fuck my ass, Daddy."

FUCK, the mouth on her. I stroke my dick as I watch her trying to stay still while the dildo fucks her perfectly round ass. "Take that cock like the pretty slut you are. Show me how badly you want it. How you crave to be used by me."

SHE SCREAMS as she moves to meet the dildo, the clamps pulling her lips. "Please, Daddy. Please put your cock in my pussy. Give your pretty whore your cum."

I PUSH my way into her cunt, making her appreciate the full extent of my magic cross invading her pussy.

"OH, my god. Why don't all men have one of those?"

I SLAP HER TIT, connecting with the clamp. "Don't you fuckin' dare think about any other man's cock while I'm buried deep in your pussy. This juicy cunt is mine. If any man comes sniffing near you, I'll slit his fuckin' throat." I pull at the chain of the clamps, and she screams. "Do you understand me?"

. . .

"Yes, Daddy. It's your pussy. Only yours."

I RAM my cock in her tight cunt and make her scream as I pull the clothespins from her lips in one tug. I turn on the vibration of the dildo as I fuck her with abandon.

"God, Daddy, I'm so full."

I WRAP my hand around her throat, grabbing forcefully. "Open your mouth, slut." I force my fingers into her mouth, pulling her lips away from her face, distorting it. "I'm going to drown you in cum. Drench this pussy, your ass, your face. Make you my perfect slut. I'm going to make you walk around with my jizz on your face so everyone knows exactly who you belong to. So they can smell me on you, know I've marked you. You hear me, whore? I'm going to make you my pathetic cum dump. Is that what you want, Solnce? To be drenched in Daddy's cum?"

"Yes. I'm nothing but a fuck hole for you to use, Daddy. That's all I want to be. A good little whore for you."

"So fuckin' tight. I'm not going to last long. Your pussy is milking my cock so well, pretty girl. Where do you want my cum?"

"I want you to fill me. I want to know you were in me, that you own this pussy. Make me yours, Alexie. Come in me."

Her dirty talk has me on edge. My balls tighten as my chest constricts. This woman doesn't just own my dick, she owns my fuckin' heart. I grunt, leaning down, taking her lips with mine, pouring my emotions into that gentle caress as my cock brutally invades her pussy. My lips meet hers with the force of the ocean and the sun. A kiss that makes me long to wrap her in every emotion I have for her. I'm darkness, and she's my light.

I WAS DROWNING, and this woman saved me. I have a reason to fight. She's given me a reason to want more than the blackness of night. She's given me hope. For the first time in a long time, I don't long for the stillness of night but crave the sun's warmth.

I KISS her as if her lips are my only lifeline to sanity, to humanity. My hands glide over her curves, skimming the hills and valleys of her body before I meet her bound hands. My fingers move through the knots as I undo them. I want her free. I crave her touch.

HER ARMS FALL AROUND ME, and she embraces me. Her hips move to meet mine. Sharp nails dig at my back, letting me know the pleasure I'm giving her. I welcome the pain because it's no longer about the torture of feeling something. With her, it's about learning to live.

A GROAN SLIPS from my lips as I spill into her, claiming her as mine.

"I NEVER KNEW sex could be like that," she whispers against my lips.

MY LIPS BRUSH the tip of her nose as I move down her body. My cock is still deep in her sweet pussy. I pull out of her slowly, bending down. My cum slips out of her slowly. I move it back into her cunt before spreading a small dollop on her sweet clit. "Keep your legs up. I don't want a drop of my cum to fall out of your pussy."

WHITE LIQUID PEEKS out of her cunt, and the dildo's still lodged up her thick ass as I undo the spreader bar at her knees. Releasing her legs from their restraints, I push them toward her head. "Grab on to your ankles and keep your ass elevated.

She does as I ask without complaint. Her succulent pussy presented to me like a gourmet meal. Like an animal, I barrel down on her cunt, my lips closing around her hole as I lick our juices into my mouth as if it's the elixir of life.

"Fuckin' delicious," I mumble into her cunt as I gorge on her, taking us in.

I suck at her sweet hole and lick my way up to her clit, placing two fingers in her pussy and pressing on her G-spot. Her body trembles, telling me she's close, so close. My hand roams to her lower abdomen, and I push down.

"What are you doing, Alexie? I'm- I'm going to pee. Stop, stop. I have to pee."

. . .

I ignore her demands, knowing she'll blow, releasing liquid from her cunt, but it won't be urine. I chuckle, ensuring my tongue doesn't move from her sweet spot. My fingers and hand apply pressure at their stations as her hips buck, and she drenches my face.

"That's a good girl, giving Daddy your sweet juice to quench his thirst."

12

MIA

"DRINK," Alexie demands, holding an open bottle of water to my lips.

"I'M NOT THIRSTY."

"IT DOESN'T MATTER if you're thirsty. Drink."

I TURN MY HEAD AWAY, frustrated at the bossy nature of this man.

HE GROWLS, yanking my hair back. My mouth opens to protest, and he spits the clear water from his mouth into mine. "The sex we have requires that you're well cared for. That means you need food and water in your body. I won't allow you to go hungry or be dehydrated, ever. You hear me? If I have to, I'll tie you up again and force it down your throat. Now, you're gonna be a good girl. Sit up, drink your water, and eat the food I've placed in front of you. If you decide to act out, I'll take it out on your sexy little ass. I don't want to punish you, Mia, but I will if it's for your own good."

THIS MAN IS INSUFFERABLE. My fingers claw into his arms, and he moans. My upper body rises, and I bring my face to his shoulders before I bite down. "You seem to forget that I bite back."

· · ·

ALEXIE'S humorless laugh echoes through the room. The sound is deranged. He grabs my throat, his thumb rubbing my hot skin. He's warning me, letting me know that no matter how much I think I'm in charge, I'm nothing more than his prey.

HIS GRAY EYES APPEAR SINISTER, and his smile looks lascivious. "You want it rough, baby doll? You want Daddy to show you what kind of monster he can be?" His eyes move down my body to my erect nipples, reacting to his words like some cheap hussy. Alexie smiles, and before I can say anything, he flips me around, holding me still.

I SHOULD TELL him to stop, but foolishly I don't.

HE BENDS ME OVER, holding my head toward the mattress. His fingers probe me to check how wet I am before he pounds his cock into me. His thrusts aren't loving or gentle. They're the thrusts of an animal, a man who doesn't care about anything other than showing his brute dominance.

BLINDING pain shoots through my scalp as his other hand yanks my hair back. I want to scream, but his fingers quickly find their way around my throat, making it impossible.

"YOU WANT TO BE A BRAT, slut? You want to make me fuck you like an animal? To bring you to your knees? You've unleashed the monster, baby. Now you'll understand what it means to disobey me."

MY ENTIRE BODY bursts into molten lava as he sinks his teeth into my shoulder. Sharp pain shoots into my flesh. Blood trickles down my chest, moving to the slopes of my breasts.

.   .   .

ONE HAND REMAINS on my throat while the other moves through my pussy as his fingers play with my clit like an acclaimed guitarist plucking at his strings. The way Alexie takes control of my body is nothing short of masterful. It's as if he knows every nerve ending and desire in my mind and uses the knowledge to convert me into his subject.

"YOU LIKE THIS SLUT? You must because your dirty cunt is drenched. I'm an animal to you, Mia, the monster, but you're the one with all the control, and that makes you wet. You crave the idea of taming the beast. It's what you need, knowing you've brought a man like me to his knees. You like knowing it's this sexy body, your voice, your smoky eyes, the way sweat glistens on your pretty skin. Every fuckin' thing about you makes my cock hard. I may be the one who takes control, who manipulates you in the bedroom, but you, slut, are the one who's manipulated my heart because I'm not walking away at the end of our bargain. I fuckin' can't."

. . .

HIS WORDS ARE TRUE, and I can't deny them. I'm lost in the rapture of him. I crave his depravity like I crave air. I'm not sure how I can go on living without this. Maybe this situation is fucked up, but I've finally gotten something I've never had with Alexie.

HE'S GIVEN ME CONTROL.

MY BODY CONVULSES as he pulls me to his chest, holding me like I'm precious, and if he lets go, all of this will be nothing but a fevered dream. "Come for me, Mia. Come all over my big fat cock. Show Daddy how much you love being fucked like the dirty whore we know you are. Be a perfect slut and do as you're told."

MY FINGERS DIG into his arms as he continues his onslaught in my pussy with his magical cock and my clit with his combustible fingers. My body folds for him, and I scream my orgasm. "I'm coming! Jesus, I'm coming!"

. . .

HE GRIPS MY THROAT, bringing his mouth to my ear. "Jesus walked on water, baby, but it was my cock that made you beg for the devil."

13

A Maxie

EVEN WATCHING her put food in her damn mouth is fucking sexy. I'm lost in the knowledge that a woman could be this perfect for me. I'm as happy eating beside her as I was fucking her brains out.

"OH, GOD, THAT'S SO GOOD," she moans as I rub her wrists.

I MAKE a mental note not to tie them so hard next time. I don't like the marks imprinted on her skin from the rope. "I'm sorry."

"WHAT ARE YOU SORRY FOR?"

"I SHOULD'VE THOUGHT about the marks on your wrists."

SHE SMIRKS, pointing her index finger at the vicious teeth marks on her shoulders and neck. "You're remorseful about that, but not about these?"

"I MEANT TO DO THOSE. The wrist was because I was careless, and I never want to be careless with you."

HER BREATH HITCHES, and she abruptly pulls her arm out of my grasp. "Don't say words you don't mean."

.   .   .

"I don't."

"Everyone says things they don't mean. Everyone puts on a mask in the beginning, but then the outer shell peels away, and the truth is revealed."

Rage rolls through me. I don't like the wall she's building between us. I take one step forward with her, she shoots me out of her atmosphere, and I need to find my way back to step one all over again. My instinct is to grab her and turn her ass red, shove my cock in her pussy until the endorphins of sex put her at my mercy again. But I realize that won't give me what I need from her. I need her secrets. Without them, I'll never get her heart.

I roll off the bed, my feet hitting the cold hardwood, and walk to her side. Dropping to my knees, I frame her pretty face with my hands, forcing her eyes to meet mine. "I don't know what happened in the past. But I know what I feel. I don't want to hurt you, Mia. All I want is to love you. My love might be scary. It may be erratic and feral, but it's also protective and loyal. You never need to be frightened of me. I'd rather slit my throat than hurt you. What we do in the bedroom isn't meant to abuse you. It brings us closer and connects us on a deeper level. That's why you have a safe word. I'm insane, but I'm also capable of loving with the depth of an ocean. You need to trust me, even if it's a drop."

SHE TILTS her head back and focuses on some imaginary spot on the ceiling. "I have a hard time with men. Sex is simple. I can give up my body, but other parts of me? Well, that's a different story."

"GET UP." I lift her, and the food I ordered sloshes off the bed.

. . .

SHE GRABS the open water bottle before it spills all over the thousand thread count sheets. "What? Why? Where are we going?"

"I AM GOING to take a shower with the most beautiful woman I've ever seen, so if the reaper comes for me tonight, I'll die a fortunate man."

SHE ROLLS HER EYES, but a giggle escapes her sexy, full lips. "You planning on offing yourself tonight?"

I SHRUG. "YOU NEVER KNOW."

"WAIT, I don't have a cap, and I need my wrap. I can't get my hair wet. I need things."

I SMILE and point to the second bag that came with the food. "I got what you need. I'll always get you what you need."

. . .

SHE TILTS HER HEAD, and her eyes narrow. Walking to the reusable bag sitting by the St. Andrew's Cross, she peers inside. Her soft eyes glisten with moisture as she looks back at me, and her lips curve into a smile. "When did you get all this?" She pulls out a white silk pillowcase, a crimson silk bonnet, and a plastic shower cap.

I WALK TOWARD HER, cupping her head in my hands, and place a gentle kiss on her forehead. "When I ordered the food."

I WRAP my fingers around hers, a simple act that means more to me than I could ever put into words. In all my thirty years, I've never held another woman's hand except my mother's. She died when I was a child, but that's a story for another time.

WE MOVE INTO THE BATHROOM, and all I can focus on is Mia. How fuckin' breathtaking she is, how strong, how beautiful, and how even if she doesn't realize it yet, she's mine.

MY HAND MOVES to her tight spaghetti strap top, and my fingers shake as I open the buttons.

"WAIT," she whispers, placing her hand on top of mine. "I'll shower alone."

"THE FUCK YOU WILL. I want to see every inch of this sexy body. I want to see that sexy stomach, explore it with my hands and tongue. You will not keep that from me."

"IT'S NOT THAT. IT'S..." Her voice trails off.

I BEND so she's forced to look at me. "It's what, Mia?"

.   .   .

SHE DOESN'T ANSWER ME. I should be patient, but I grip the fabric at both ends and tear it open viciously. Time, space, and everything in between stops. Violent slashes crisscross her skin.

"WHO DID THIS TO YOU?" I ask slowly, enunciating each word, making each syllable as clear as crystal.

SHE USES her hands to cover herself, and I let her. I grip her shoulders and turn her to see a carving in big, bold letters.

ROBERT'S BITCH.

14

M_{IA}

"WHO'S ROBERT," Alexie asks, his voice cold, void of any emotion but anger. The softness in his eyes is gone, replaced by venom.

I MOVE AWAY FROM HIM, one small step at a time, and he matches my stride until my back is against the cool wall.

"I ASKED YOU A QUESTION, Mia. Who the fuck is Robert?"

"MY EX."

"THE SAME PIECE of shit who told you that you weren't attractive?"

I NOD as Alexie barrels out of the bathroom, muttering profanities under his breath. I chase after him and watch in horror as he tosses on his clothes. Grabbing the sheet off the bed, I wrap it around myself, desperately wanting to hide my shame and bring back the way he looked at me a moment ago.

HE GLARES AT ME. "What are you doing?"

"I ASSUME you're disgusted by me. That you want nothing more to do with me?"

. . .

"AFTER I KILL THE FUCKER, I'll be back to spank your ass raw for that statement."

"WHAT DO YOU MEAN?"

"I TOLD you I was going to kill the motherfucker, but now? Now, I'm going to gut him like a fish."

THE SHEET POOLS at my feet as I move frantically through the room, finding my discarded clothing and tossing them on haphazardly.

"WHAT ARE YOU DOING?" Alexie asks.

"I'M NOT STANDING for this. If you want to go around killing people, I'm not gonna be here when you come back."

. . .

BEFORE I CAN MOVE, my back's slammed against the wall and his fingers are wrapped around my throat. His voice is low and barely human, an animalistic growl. "You seem to be under the illusion I'm a good guy, Solnce. Far from it. I'm a living nightmare. You're sorely mistaken if you believe I'd let some man mark up my woman. If you expect to get a say in how I deal with a problem like that, you're dead wrong. I'm going to kill the fucker, and afterward, I'm coming back to fuck you while I'm still covered in his blood."

"YOU'RE FUCKIN' crazy."

"I KNOW, but you like it. You enjoy knowing I'm so fucked up I'd burn the entire world down for you. Knowing you matter so much to me that I'd kill my brother for you is thrilling. My obsession with you is thicker than blood, and that's what will keep you with me. Always."

. . .

As much as I hate his words, not one thing he said is a lie. "I'm coming with you."

"You can come, but you can't stop me. So make sure you're coming because you want to see me get rid of the problem. He touched what's mine, and now, he's a dead man walking."

"I wasn't yours then," I protest.

"No, Solnce, you were always mine. We didn't know it until now." Alexie brushes his fingers across my cheek before placing a kiss on my lips. "Let's go."

"Alexie, what does Solnce mean?"

"It's Russian for sunshine."

.   .   .

"WHY DO YOU CALL ME THAT?"

"BECAUSE I WAS LIVING in perpetual frost before you. You are the warmth I'd always been seeking."

"I NEED TO REMEMBER THIS MOMENT."

"WHY?"

I LOOK at him and smile. "It's the moment you cracked my heart."

15

Maxie

ROBERT MONTGOMERY IS a piece of shit, accountant who wears the camouflage of a nerdy, nice guy. I called Kian, and he ran a background check on him. No family apart from a grandmother in Florida who has Alzheimer's.

I DON'T EVEN BOTHER KNOCKING on his door, kicking it down and walking straight in as if I own the place.

"WHO THE FUCK ARE YOU?" Robert demands as he barrels toward us.

HE DOESN'T SAY another word. I wrap my hand around his throat and slam him down on the hardwood floor. I'm not careful with him like I am with my Solnce. I squeeze so tight that his eyes almost bulge out of his head. "The grim reaper, motherfucker."

I PULL out the knife from my pocket and drag it along the buttons of his shirt. They pop open and expose his bare chest. He tries to speak, but my hold on his throat doesn't allow him to utter a word.

I drag the sharp tip of the blade from his chin down his bare chest. "You like cutting women, Robert? Does it make you feel like a big man?"

· · ·

HIS GAZE ROAMS to the door, and recognition flashes in his petrified eyes as he spots Mia. I stab his stomach. "Don't you dare look at her, motherfucker."

"LYING," he spits.

BEFORE I CAN SAY ANYTHING, Mia's heels connect with his right eye, moving straight into his head. She tears off her shirt, exposing the vicious lines along her stomach. "I'm lying about this?" She turns, exposing the jagged letters on her back. "*I* carved your name into my back, did I, asshole? *I* did this to myself? Why? So I can walk around hating my body? So I was scared to ever fuck another man under a light?" She pulls her heel out and jabs him in the face, his blood spurting. "The only piece of shit liar here is you."

I PULL off my belt and tie his hands together before I stand and tug Mia away from him.

· · ·

"GET OFF ME!" she shouts.

"SOLNCE. You'll get your revenge, but if I let you keep going, you're gonna kill him before we have a chance to make him suffer."

MY WORDS HAVE the effect I want. She stops stabbing his face with her heel and spits on him before turning to me. "I want him to suffer. I want him to know every bit of humiliation and pain he caused me."

MY HANDS MOVE through her hair, and I pull her toward me, crushing my lips to hers. I taste her tears and frustration, and my cock gets rock hard for her. I'm a sick fuck because as much as I love this woman, I also love suffering and pain. Love. The realization is not lost on me. I love Solnce. I pull away and stare at her beautiful face before turning my attention back to the piece of shit who thought he could lay a hand on my woman.

· · ·

I HAUL Robert up and shove him into the bedroom, tossing him on his bed.

Mia frowns. "What are we doing in here?"

I BEND Mia over the bed and pull down her pants, unzipping mine and freeing my hard cock.

"REALLY?" she asks.

I DON'T SAY a word as I hand her the knife. "Every time my cock moves in and out of your cunt, I want you to stab him. I want to pound your tight pussy while you bathe in his blood."

MY FINGERS BRUSH HER CUNT, and she's drenched. I smile before I push my way in, and Robert screams as the knife slides into his stomach. Bending down I grab a discarded underwear off the floor. Robert shakes his head, but I plug his nose forcing his mouth open before I shove the fabric inside. "That should keep the noise down."

HIS HEAD SLUMPS, he's obviously losing blood, but Mia is stabbing him in places that will keep him alive. At least for now.

"Tell him how good my cock is. Tell him he was never good at keeping your cunt satisfied like my thick dick."

"THIS IS A REAL MAN, Robbie. His cock is long and thick, and when he's in my pussy, I think he might split me open with his size. Your cock was so small that I wondered if you were inside me. Barely three inches and thin as a toothpick."

I LAUGH. "Is that why you hurt her, Robert? Because you never knew how to satisfy her cunt? You weren't man enough?"

. . .

ROBERT IS COVERED IN BLOOD, he can barely speak. His words come out jumbled, but he still wants to prove he's something other than trash. "Fuck you! She's a pathetic whore."

"THIS TIME when you stab him, Solnce, twist the knife."

I HAMMER INTO MIA, over and over, forcing her to stab Robert constantly until his body slumps. "Stop stabbing him, baby. I need him alive for the grand finale."

I RUB HER CLIT, and she moans. "Keep fucking me, Alexie. I'm so close."

I KEEP my pace on her clit and hold the rhythm of my cock in her pussy. "Come all over my cock, baby."

"FUCK, I'M COMING."

. . .

I PULL OUT OF HER, not wanting to cum in her pussy. I walk over to Robert yanking his head back; his eyes gaze up at me with fear and horror. Directing my dick towards him, I release my cum all over his face.

"This is her cum on my dick, Robert. You weren't man enough to keep her, so I should thank you." I grab the knife from Mia. "But you also weren't man enough not to hurt her, and for that, I'm going to kill you." I push the knife into his heart and twist, watching the light fade from his eyes.

"REST IN PISS, MOTHERFUCKER."

A Mixie

"YOU READY," I ask as I kiss along her collarbone.

HER BLACK SHIRT IS BACKLESS, and I smile at the large tattoo of a phoenix, wings wide open as it flies over flames that replaces her scars. Doctor Mia Fedorov has come a long way since we met ten years ago. She's an up-and-coming cardiologist, a wife, and still the sexiest woman I've ever seen.

"You ready, Solnce?"

She turns, adjusting her mask before fixing mine. "I'm a little nervous. I'm not sure if I'm ready for this."

She wanted to show herself off, be sexy and proud of everything she's gone through, and what better way to do it than to fuck her husband in front of a room full of people.

I place the thick leather collar around her neck, securing the leash. "You're so fuckin' hot." I move her hand to my cock so she knows how hard I am for her.

She smirks. "Down, boy. We've got a show to put on."

. . .

I PULL her to me and kiss her. "My sexy little whore."

"YES, BABY, YOURS. ALL YOURS."

"YOU SURE YOU WANT THE COLLAR?" I pull at the chain.

"YES, I want everyone to realize I'm yours. That I belong to you."

SHE SMILES as I tug at her leash and walk out the door of our room at the club toward the main floor. We stand at the entrance, looking out at the crowd. Different people in many sex acts. A man getting flogged by a domina-trix, a woman having a train being run up on her, a line-up of men waiting to fuck her and dump a load on her body. A man bent over with two cocks in his mouth while his wife is being fucked by a man with a foot-long cock.

"Show time, slut." I walk into the room, holding onto Mia's leash.

WE WALK TO THE STAGE, and I place Mia at one end while I walk to the other. I put a purple dildo on the table before removing my jacket and discarding it.

MIA SMILES at me right before I order, "On your knees, slut. Crawl to Daddy like a good little whore."

SHE MOVES LIKE A GAZELLE, so elegant and beautiful. The weighted nipple clamps on her full tits jiggle with every move she makes. I rub my crotch, and my mouth waters. She's so damn beautiful. My eyes roam the crowd, and the room quiets as they watch my sexy wife crawl like the good girl she is.

I MADE her wear a shirt with only sleeves and a scoop neck to hold it in place. I love how her belly hangs down. It's the sexiest part of her body. It's a place she didn't like for a long time, but now she embraces the body I worship like it's the tabernacle.

WHEN SHE REACHES ME, I pet her head, and she falls into my caress. My thumb glides along her lips, and she parts them in an erotic sigh.

"SUCH A PRETTY GIRL." I push my thumb between her lips, forcing her to open her mouth before I add more fingers. "Are you ready to be a good whore for Daddy and make him proud?"

SHE NODS HER HEAD.

MY OTHER HAND moves to her mouth, and I use my fingers to separate her lips before I bend and spit in her mouth. "Such a good girl."

. . .

I TUG AT THE CHAIN, forcing her to her feet, and move her to the table. "Bend over and present your ass to Daddy."

AS SOON AS she's in position, I rip her fishnet stockings so I have access to her two sexy holes. My fingers dip into her cunt. "So wet, baby. Does it turn you on knowing all these people are going to watch you get railed like a filthy whore?"

"YES," she pants.

"THAT'S MY GOOD GIRL," I say as I push the dildo into her pussy, moving it in and out. "I'm going to stretch my cunt nice and wide today. I'm going to make your gape so large that I'll be able to get both my fists in this pussy. I'm going to make you feel like the dirty whore we know you are."

· · ·

SHE'S SO FUCKIN' wet that the dildo slides out of her cunt.

"PLEASE, DADDY," she begs, "I need you to use me. Make me your perfect whore."

"I DON'T HAVE to make you do anything, baby. You are and always will be my perfect slut."

She shivers as I brush the tip of my cock to her entrance and slowly push it in.

MIA

"MY EYES WATCH the crowd as my husband pushes his cock further into me, joining the dildo. "Oh, god," I moan, taking it all.

I JERK as his hand connects with my ass. "Tell everyone how sexy you are. Tell them you have the best pussy on the planet, and they are not good enough to get a taste."

. . .

"WHAT?" I ask, shocked at his demands.

ALEXIE SLAPS my ass again before rubbing my cheek. "You heard me, my pretty slut. Tell them how good and tight this cunt of mine is."

"ALEXIE, DON'T BE LUDICROUS." I scream as he pinches my clit, hard.

HIS HOT BREATH is on my ear. "Do it, or I will belt your clit until it bleeds."

MY BODY SHIVERS at his threat, not from fear but from pure lust. Alexie will do it. Over the years, he's taken a belt to me many times. It's helped me take control of my life in ways I didn't know were possible. Bending to his will in the bedroom has given me more confidence.

. . .

"MY LITTLE WHORE gets turned on at the idea of her daddy punishing her puffy clit?"

"YES," I admit.

"YOU SHOULD REFUSE my request so I can punish you like you want."

'OH, God, are you trying to kill me by making me wet beyond reason?"

ALEXIE CHUCKLES. "You know how much I enjoy watching you come from pain. I want you to refuse me so I can make your clit puffy and red. I should make you suck my cock while I do it."

JESUS, this man was taking it to another level tonight. I want to refuse the order, but I know tonight is about taking more control. Tonight is about finally wiping away the scars and taking it all back.

TEN YEARS AGO, I met Alexie, and my life changed forever. Tonight is about solidifying that life. I'm sure some would find being treated like this in front of a crowd demeaning, but for me, it's a taste of true freedom.

I STARE out at the crowd. "I'm a whore with two cocks in her tight little cunt. I feel like they're going to rip me apart. I'm so full. I wish I had a third dick in my ass."

ALEXIE PINCHES MY CLIT. "Good girl. You look so sexy telling everyone what a good whore you are for Daddy. Pretty whore, so fucking beautiful."

THE MIXTURE of degradation and praise has me right on the edge. "I'm gonna come, Daddy. Oh, God, I'm gonna come."

· · ·

"Come, baby. Drench me like a good girl, but make sure they all know what's happening."

My hands grope the sides of the table. "I'm coming!" I yell as my entire body ignites with my release.

Alexie quickens his pace as he keeps his finger on my clit, not giving me any reprieve from my orgasm. Building me up. The pressure is out of this world, and my body convulses again.

He pulls the dildo from my pussy, while he continues to fuck me. My mouth gapes from the pleasure he's giving me. I start to speak, but he shoves the toy in my mouth. "Show everyone what a good cock sucker you are. Make them wish it was their cock in your mouth."

I suck on the dildo like a cock, moving my mouth up and down, forcing myself to gag on it. Consuming it like it's Alexie's cock.

"You look so hot sucking on that cock, baby. So fucking sexy." His thrusts are more frequent, more forceful, the weights on my tits pinching my nipples. "I'm gonna pull out, and when I do, I want you on your knees with your mouth open and your tongue out, ready to take all my cum."

Alexie pulls out of me, and I drop to my knees like someone starved, finally receiving a scrap of food. Ropes of cum shoot out of Alexie's cock, landing on my face and tongue.

"Turn to the crowd and let them see your face covered in cum."

I turn to the crowd, and pride blooms through me. I'm desirable and powerful.

.   .   .

"So pretty painted in my cum, Solnce. So fucking sexy. Maybe I should save up my cum and make you bathe in it. Make you a proper whore." He bends down, kissing me on the top of the head. "Swallow."

I close my mouth and relish the sweet and salty taste of my husband. I look up, locking eyes with the man I love beyond all reason.

"I love you, Solnce. Hope you liked this little fantasy. But I'm never doing this again. The urge to kill everyone in this room for seeing your body is too strong."

I laugh as I pull him to me and kiss him. "You're a lunatic."

"Baby, you've known that from the moment we met. But I bet you never thought I'd be *your* lunatic."

"I love you, Alexie," I whisper.

.   .   .

"Not as much as I love you, Solnce."

Printed in Great Britain
by Amazon

84058866R00093